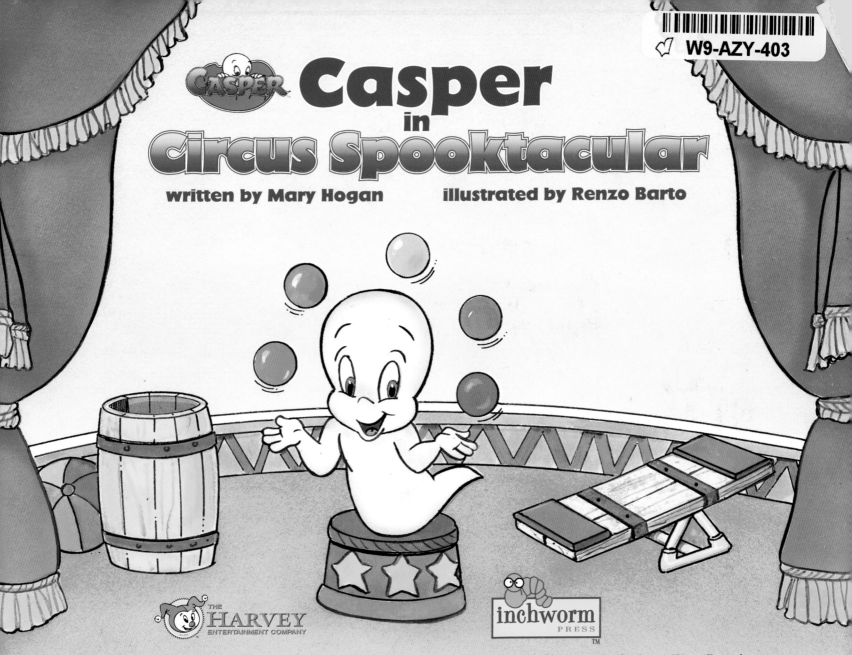

Casper
in
Circus Spooktacular

written by Mary Hogan   **illustrated by Renzo Barto**

Copyright © 1998 Harvey Comics, Inc. All Characters and Related Indicia are Trademarks of and Copyrighted by Harvey Comics, Inc. A Harvey Entertainment Company. All rights reserved. Licensed exclusively by Harvey Consumer Products. No part of this book may be reproduced without written permission from the publisher. Published in the United States by Inchworm Press, an imprint of GT Publishing Corporation, 16 E. 40th Street, New York, NY 10016.

Casper, Spooky, and Fatso visited the Circus Spooktacular.
BOOM! A cannon sent a skinny ghost whizzing through the air.
"Whew," said Casper, "good thing he landed in that cobweb safety net."

"Hooray for Boo-mer, the Un-human Cannonball!" shouted the ringmaster. "One thousand launches and no broken bones. Not that he has any bones to break!"

"Good thing this popcorn isn't as old as that joke," said Fatso, munching happily.

Spooky sighed. "This circus is boring. It should be called the Circus Snoozetacular."

Trapeze artists flipped and flew through the air.
"Oh, no," said Casper. "That ghost slipped off his swing."
Plop! The ghost landed in the slime pit—safe and sound, but stinky and sticky.

"Yuck," said Casper. "I wouldn't want to be covered with that gooey stuff."

"Mmm . . . gooey," said Fatso. He was eating cotton candy, but making such a mess that it looked like it was eating him!

"Gooey phooey," grumbled Spooky.

"Please direct your eyes to the Root 'n' Tootin' Rubber Bands!" shouted the ringmaster. "These gangly ghosts can twist and turn themselves into any shape."

"Those clowns look like a ghost pretzel," said Casper, laughing.

"Real pretzels are tastier," said Fatso, chomping on one.

Spooky yawned so widely that he looked like he was going to swallow his own hat. "I'm wasting my afterlife here," he said.

"Uh-oh, Spooky, did those clowns hear you?" asked Casper.

Whiz! Bang! Pop! The Root 'n' Tootin' Rubber Bands s-n-a-pped apart
and zoomed and zipped all over the circus.

Whee! The audience loved all the crazy careening!

"Good thing it's all part of the show," said Casper. "I thought they were going after Spooky."

"Now welcome Bitty Banshee, the littlest lion tamer ever!" cried the ringmaster.

Bitty Banshee entered the ring. She was surrounded by three ferocious ghost lions. The lions growled and paced around her, lashing with their huge claws. Unafraid, she opened her itsy-bitsy-teeny-weeny-mini-mousy mouth and let out a . . . R-O-A-R!

Shaking and quaking, the lions leaped into place.
"That lion tamer is brave," said Casper. He was impressed.
"This chocolate is tasty," said Fatso. He was impressed, too.
"Those overgrown kitties are just a bunch of scaredy cats," said Spooky.
"I came here for a good spook, and instead I'm getting a good snooze."

"Watch high in the sky!"
shouted the ringmaster.
"The Amazing Splatto
will leap from that
platform into this
giant bucket of water."

Whoosh! Down dived the Amazing Splatto—but just as he did some troublemaking clowns appeared.

"Look!" said Casper. "Those clowns are replacing Splatto's bucket with a tiny cup!"

But Fatso was more interested in looking at his bubble gum. And Spooky was more interested in looking grumpy.

SQUISH!

"Poor Splatto," said Casper. The diving ghost was stuck in the tiny cup.

"All this talk about cups is making me thirsty," announced Fatso. "I'm going to get a Cherry Fizz. Watch my peanuts, Spooky."

"Sure," answered Spooky, tipping his hat over his eyes. "Your peanuts are the most interesting thing to watch at this silly circus."

Casper wanted to boost Spooky's spirits. But what could he do?
Just then, a huge elephant plodded by. Hmm . . . Casper had the ghost of an idea.
"Hello, elephant," called Casper. "You look very hungry."

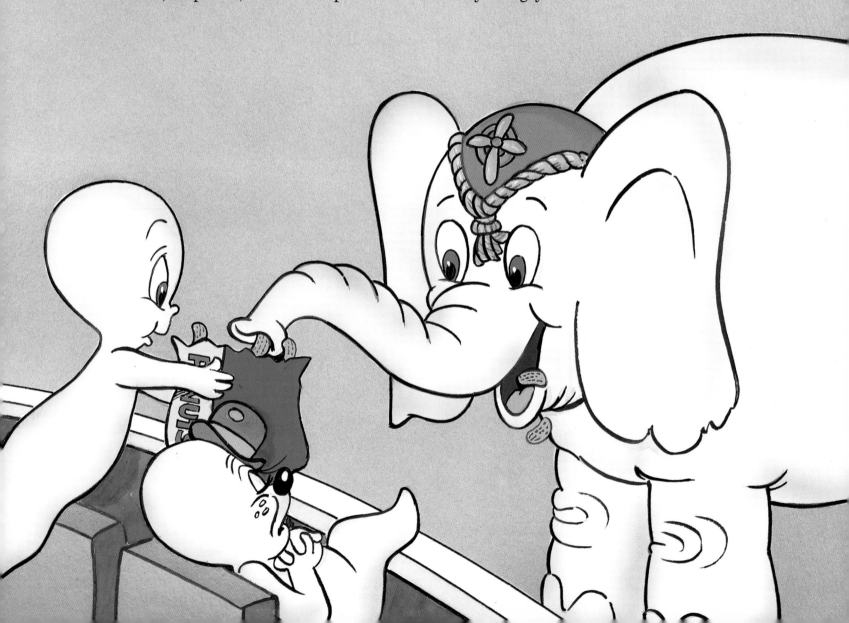

Soon the friendly elephant ate all the peanuts. Fatso returned to find an empty peanut bag and a snoozing Spooky.

"MY PEANUTS!" yelled Fatso. Spooky awoke just in time to see Fatso spinning and whirling and roaring. He was green! He was purple! He was huge and getting huger! HE BOUNCED AND BOUNDED!

He was . . . being applauded?

All the ghosts at the Circus Spooktacular were clapping. A hungry Fatso was the scariest sight of all.

"Oh, it was nothing," said Fatso, modestly. "Just hunger pangs."

Poor Spooky! He was still shivering from Fatso's scare.
"Have some hot cocoa with cinnamon, Spooky," said Casper. "It's the best thing to calm you down after a visit to the Circus Spooktacular."